Dear Parent:
Your child's love of reading starts here!

Every child learns to read in a different way and at his or her own speed. Some go back and forth between reading levels and read favorite books again and again. Others read through each level in order. You can help your young reader improve and become more confident by encouraging his or her own interests and abilities. From books your child reads with you to the first books he or she reads alone, there are I Can Read Books for every stage of reading:

SHARED READING
Basic language, word repetition, and whimsical illustrations, ideal for sharing with your emergent reader

BEGINNING READING
Short sentences, familiar words, and simple concepts for children eager to read on their own

READING WITH HELP
Engaging stories, longer sentences, and language play for developing readers

READING ALONE
Complex plots, challenging vocabulary, and high-interest topics for the independent reader

ADVANCED READING
Short paragraphs, chapters, and exciting themes for the perfect bridge to chapter books

I Can Read Books have introduced children to the joy of reading since 1957. Featuring award-winning authors and illustrators and a fabulous cast of beloved characters, I Can Read Books set the standard for beginning readers.

A lifetime of discovery begins with the magical words "I Can Read!"

Visit www.icanread.com for information
on enriching your child's reading experience.

Monsters vs. Aliens: Team Monster
Monsters vs. Aliens ™ & copyright © 2009 DreamWorks Animation L.L.C.
All rights reserved. Printed in the United States of America.
No part of this book may be used or reproduced in any manner whatsoever without written permission except
in the case of brief quotations embodied in critical articles and reviews. For information address HarperCollins Children's Books,
a division of HarperCollins Publishers, 1350 Avenue of the Americas, New York, NY 10019.
www.icanread.com

Library of Congress catalog card number: 2008942537
ISBN 978-0-06-156727-8

Typography by Rick Farley

❖

First Edition

I Can Read!

READING 2 WITH HELP

DREAMWORKS

MONSTERS VS ALIENS

TEAM MONSTER

adapted by Gail Herman
pictures by MADA Design

HarperCollins*Publishers*

Across the country,

word was spreading fast.

There was big trouble.

A giant alien robot had landed.

Nothing could stop the robot.

"Somebody do something!"

said the president to his staff.

"I have a plan!"

said General W. R. Monger.

"I've been keeping monsters
in a secret prison,"
General Monger explained,
"because people are afraid of them.
But now, they can help."

General Monger put on a video.
One by one, the faces
of five monsters filled the screens
throughout the room.

"Say hello to Insectosaurus,"
said the General.
"It used to be a small grub.
Now it's three hundred and fifty
feet tall."

"Here's B.O.B.," said the General,
"and Dr. Cockroach, PhD.
This one is The Missing Link.
He is a twenty-thousand-year-old
frozen fish-man who thawed out.
Our newest monster is a giant
named Ginormica," said the General.

The president was excited.

"Monsters versus Aliens!" he said.

"Let's do it!"

At the monster prison,

General Monger said,

"Good news, monsters!

You're getting out.

You just have to defeat a robot."

When they left the prison,

the monsters smiled.

The fresh air felt so good.

Then they saw the robot.

"I'll put a dent in that tin can!"
said The Missing Link.
But the robot was so big!
Only Ginormica could bring it down.
And she did. They were free!

Ginormica's parents threw a party.

B.O.B. talked to the pudding.

Dr. Cockroach mixed

an exploding drink.

The party did not go well.

But the trouble had just begun.

Outside a gas station

a spaceship floated low in the sky.

The ship belonged to an evil alien

named Gallaxhar.

Gallaxhar had sent the huge robot!

Now he was after the monsters.

Gallaxhar pressed a button.

A beam of light lifted Ginormica

into the air.

Insectosaurus shot its silk
to catch Ginormica.
Gallaxhar fired back.
Insectosaurus fell down
and was still.

Then Gallaxhar sent his message
around the world:
"My robots are landing.
I am taking over your planet."

"I'll tell you what we'll do,"
said The Missing Link.
"We'll get onto that alien ship!"
Quickly, the team put on jet packs.

General Monger's plane took them
close to the ship.

The General gave a salute.

"That's rude!" said B.O.B.

"That's respect!"said Dr. Cockroach.

The monsters zoomed out the door.

The monsters got to the ship. Working fast, The Missing Link turned B.O.B. into a slingshot. The Missing Link shot Dr. Cockroach right into Gallaxhar's computer.

Now Dr. Cockroach could fix
the wires and stop the attack.
But alien clones were everywhere!

The Missing Link charged the clones.

"Come on, you slimeballs," he said.

B.O.B. got blasted into little bits.

But the bits rolled back together.

Dr. Cockroach rewired the computer.
Gallaxhar's clones were stopped!

Gallaxhar was still on the loose
and fighting back.

Punches flew and lasers fired.

Then Ginormica trapped Gallaxhar.

"It's over!" she said.

But the ship was cracking

from all the fighting.

Sparks flew and steam hissed.

Everything was about to explode.

How would the monsters escape?

"Need a lift?" asked General Monger,
flying up on Insectosaurus's back.
Insectosaurus hadn't been hurt.
She had turned into a butterfly!

The monsters smiled and climbed

onto Insectosaurus, too.

Together, they had done it!

The world was safe.

"Thank you," said the president.

People everywhere cheered.

No one thought the monsters

were scary anymore.

They were a team of heroes.